TWISTED DEVOTION

BY KITA LASHAUN

Published by Jus King Publications

Chicago, IL.

Edited by Cayce Berryman

Cover design by Open Mic Production

Printed in the United States of America.

Acknowledgements

First and foremost, I want to thank God for blessing me with a talent I am able to share with others.

Thank you to my beautiful children Aaron, Jasmine, and Josiah for being my motivations for everything I do. I live for you all and I love you three very much. To my mother Thelma, thank you for always being there for me in EVERY way possible. My beautiful cousin Nica, you were the one who told me years ago to stop sitting on my talent and go forth with a book. So to you, my sister/cuzzy, I say thank you girl! Thank you to Kevin Winston...my partner in crime, my better half. You've been nothing but my backbone during this whole process. I can't thank you enough. Rae, thanks for looking fabulous on my cover! Last, but definitely not least, I want to thank all of you who believed in me and supported me since day one. Without you all, this would not be possible.

I hope that I continue to receive everyone's love and support, as this is only the beginning! Thank you!

Chapter I

Blinded By Love

Chrissy opened her eyes and looked at the sun shining through the curtains. Her boyfriend remained sound asleep...the perfect start to her day.

"Wake up baby," Chrissy said, nudging Steve with her foot, as she pinned her hair back. "Time for you to go to work."

Steve rose from bed and let out a long yawn. He stretched his arms and kissed Chrissy on her forehead.

"We still on for lunch?" Chrissy asked.

Steve nodded.

Chrissy removed the covers from her legs and reached over to the nightstand, grabbing her phone. After checking her voicemail, she headed to the kitchen in his studio apartment. She grabbed some bacon and eggs out of the refrigerator and began preparing his breakfast. Chrissy was feeling good. She had a great night with her man, and the sex was even greater.

As the bacon sizzled in the frying pan, Steve came into the kitchen fully dressed.

"Ah no time for breakfast Chrissy, but I'll see you later," he said.

"But I'm almost done."

Steve grabbed his jacket from the back of the chair and headed out.

Chrissy stood in his kitchen with a puzzled look on her face. Nevertheless, she wasn't going to let that ruin her morning. She ate the bacon that she had cooked, got dressed, and decided to head home and get ready for work herself.

On the way home, Chrissy's head bobbed to the radio. They were playing all her favorite artists today: Luther Vandross, Freddie Jackson, and Gerald Levert.

Chrissy tapped her thumb against the steering wheel while the radio's sound filled her car. She felt good, as she always had after a night with Steve, but she found herself more concerned than anything when they had to separate for the day. He'd shown her many things, including how to open up, and she had. She just couldn't help the nagging feeling.

Chrissy hurried to the door when she pulled up to her apartment. She fumbled with her keys, dropping them each time she tried unlocking it. After what seemed to be an eternity, she took a deep breath and was finally successful at getting inside. Her roommate sat on the couch eating popcorn and watching *Maury*.

"Bitch you couldn't open the door? I know you heard me struggling with my keys! Hell I'm late for work!"

"Um while you yelling at me, you need to be blaming yourself for being late. You was probably with Steve ol' no good ass," Keisha fired back.

Steve was known as a two-timing womanizer in his old neighborhood. Keisha warned Chrissy about him before she got in deep, but Chrissy wouldn't hear of it.

"Girl mind yo' business. You just mad because you can't find nobody!" she laughed.

"Girl bye!" Keisha replied, throwing a kernel of popcorn at her.

"Don't nobody need a man if they gon' be like Steve trifling ass!"

Chrissy jumped in the shower. As the water trickled down her body, she smiled at last night's events. Steve was the only guy to ever make her have an orgasm. He was her first true love, and she adored everything about him. From the way he held her, to the surprise gifts he lavished her with, Steve could do no wrong in her eyes.

Chrissy got dressed and headed out, making the short drive to work.

"Hey Joyce," she said when she walked in. "Curtis, how are you doing? What's up Richie?"

Chrissy's coworkers greeted her in return. When the twelve o'clock hour hit, she called Steve to see where they would meet up for lunch as planned. After three failed attempts, Chrissy decided to go to lunch alone.

****

Chrissy sat in her room after work, still waiting to hear from Steve. Hours had passed, but he had yet to return her call from before lunch. She cut the TV on to try to take her mind off him. She'd moped through the rest of her workday after returning from lunch. She didn't even remember what she'd eaten. Keisha asked Chrissy if she wanted to go grab a bite to eat, but she declined.

"Ugh, what's wrong with you? You have been acting funny ever since you got home from work," Keisha said.

"Nothing. I'm good. Just not hungry."

"Since when are you not hungry?" Keisha asked. "But ok girl, I'll be back in a little while."

"And I'll be here."

Chrissy threw the remote on her nightstand. She grabbed her Icee, slurped on it, and watched TV until she fell asleep.

The next morning, she woke up and saw that Steve had texted her.

"What's up baby? Sorry I missed your calls yesterday. My phone was tweaking. Hit me up when you get this message."

"Yeah whatever," she said, as she threw her phone back onto her nightstand.

But whom was Chrissy kidding? She couldn't ignore his texts. She grabbed her phone again and texted Steve, telling him it was okay and that she wanted to see him later. He replied, saying he would have to get with her on the weekend because he had a lot of work to do for his job. Chrissy was upset, but she understood Steve's position. Working for a huge company like his, she knew he had to be compliant. So she sucked it up and went on about her day.

Because Chrissy didn't have to work, she decided to do some cleaning around the apartment. She turned on her stereo and started with her room. She swept her floor, dusted her dresser off, and folded clothes, all while dancing to her favorite music.

She was startled by a knock on her door and stopped mid-shimmy before anyone saw. Keisha came into her room and told her to turn her music down.

"Girl you know I can't function without my dusties!" Chrissy said.

"Yeah but I can't hear *Maury*! Girl, the lady on there is about to find out if dude she been messing with is her baby daddy!"

Chrissy laughed. "Now, you know damn well he ain't gon be the daddy. Then her dumb ass is gonna run off the stage, go to that couch in the back, fall on it, and cry!"

Keisha laughed with her.

"Yeah Chrissy you might be right!"

"No Keisha girl. I am right!"

When Keisha stopped laughing, she asked Chrissy if she wanted to go to a Sip and Paint party later on.

Chrissy said, "Sure."

"Wait. You said yes?" Keisha asked. "Hell I'm shocked! You always tell me no. Steve must've dissed yo' ass tonight."

"No boo! He did not diss me. He has a lot of work to do for his job."

"Mmhm." Keisha rocked her weight onto her hip and held her hands on her waist. "Just be ready by eight thirty because it starts at nine forty-five."

****

Chrissy and Keisha pulled up to an extravagant, well-lit building. Fancy cars were parked alongside a beautifully sculptured water fountain. Keisha parked next to the cars and the girls made their way inside.

As they climbed the swirling staircase, which led to glass double doors, Chrissy and Keisha looked at one another in shock.

"This building is off the chain," Chrissy whispered. "How do you know these people?"

"You know I know people that know people," Keisha whispered back. "Now come on. Let's go check it out."

After the doorman greeted them, they were ushered down a long, red-carpeted hallway, which led to a huge room. The girls couldn't believe their eyes. All Keisha saw were dollar signs in the way people held themselves, dressed to match the status they probably had.

Keisha led the way to their seats. Their names were next to canvases, which made Chrissy feel kind of VIP.

"Look girl, we special! We got our names by our shit!"

"Look around girl. Everybody does," Keisha said.

Chrissy shrugged her shoulders.

Chrissy and Keisha sipped and painted the night away. Guests around them talked with one another, security walked the premises, and hosts scouted around to make sure everyone had what they needed. Chocolate covered strawberries were brought around to the guests, as well as raffle tickets.

"Hmm. I wonder what the prize is gonna be for the raffle winner," Chrissy said when a woman gave them tickets.

" I don't know, but I hope it's me because I'm taking whatever they giving away!"

Chrissy shoved her.

"Save the ratchetness for the house Keisha."

Keisha giggled and continued painting her picture. It was almost 11:00 p.m. Both girls were tipsy. Although they had been there a while, guests were still arriving. Keisha looked around the room at the new guests walking in.

"Chrissy let's go look around the building!"

"Girl no! We gon' get in trouble. We can't just walk around on people's property!"

Keisha gave Chrissy the side eye. Just as Chrissy thought she had gotten through to her best friend, Keisha waved down an approaching waiter.

"Excuse me sir? Can you point me in the direction of the restroom? My friend has to pee really bad, but she's a little shy. Leave it up to her, she would pee all over y'all floor! You feel me?"

Chrissy turned red. With wide eyes and a slight smile tugging at the corner of his mouth, a confused look on his face, the waiter told Keisha that the restroom was out the door and upstairs to the right.

As Keisha and Chrissy left, Chrissy slapped Keisha on the back of her head.

"Why would you do that?" Keisha asked.

"Because you so damn ignorant! Let's just find the bathroom so we can get back in time for the raffle!"

Chrissy walked up the staircase and headed to the restroom with Keisha right behind her. They could not believe how gorgeous the bathroom was. A crystal chandelier hung above every bathroom stall, and every toilet was brass.

"Well since you lied to the waiter, I might as well pee since I'm in here."

"Go ahead. I'll just be right here checking myself out in this mirror!"

Keisha fixed her hair, applied more mascara, and pulled out her phone to Snapchat while she waited on Chrissy. A lady came into the restroom. Keisha would be lying to herself if she didn't admit how beautiful she was. As Keisha adored her glittery dress, the lady spoke, making Keisha meet her gaze.

"Hello. How are you?"

"I'm fine. You?"

"I'm good. This building is so nice isn't it?"

"Yes. Yes it is," Keisha answered. "You know anyone here?"

"Not really. Just my significant other. I came with him," the lady said. "Well, nice meeting you. Maybe I'll see you around."

As she left, Keisha stared at how bad the lady's body was. She then looked down at her stomach.

"Damn. I guess I need to hit the gym," she thought.

Chrissy came out of the stall and washed her hands. Keisha didn't skip a beat, talking about the fancy woman's dress.

"Girl it was all glittery and shit! Bitch was bad! Make me wanna hit the gym."

Chrissy shook her head but didn't respond. As they prepared to head back to the Sip and Paint room, Keisha saw the pretty lady exiting the room next to the restroom.

"Look Chrissy. There she is. I told you her dress is bad!"

Keisha caught the attention of the lady and pulled Chrissy toward her. She introduced them.

"I'm sorry. I don't think I caught your name. I'm Keisha and this is my best friend Chrissy."

"Hi Chrissy. Nice to meet you. I'm Laura."

Chrissy shook her hand.

"Nice to meet you, too."

The three of them talked for a few minutes. Keisha didn't hesitate to compliment her dress. Laura smiled and said her aunt was a seamstress, which was why her dress fit every curve of her body.

Laura admitted that if it weren't for her fiancée, she wouldn't look half as good as she did.

"Okay check you out! You about to be a married woman, huh?" Keisha asked.

"Yes, that's my heart. We've been together for six years. It's definitely had its ups and downs, but I wouldn't trade him for anything. Let me introduce you girls. I'll go get him," Laura said. "Be right back!"

When Laura went into the room she'd just left, Chrissy looked at Keisha.

"Why you looking at me like that?"

"Bitch, you didn't tell me she was white!" Chrissy answered.

"Oh. My bad."

Laura walked toward them again, looking lazily around the hallway.

"I don't know where he went. But...Oh there he is!"

When Chrissy turned around, she saw Steve heading toward Laura. When he saw Chrissy, he froze.

"What's wrong baby?" Laura asked him. "Come here. Let me introduce you to these women."

Keisha spoke up. "Naw you ain't gotta introduce us. We already know who he is!"

Laura stood there perplexed. Before the woman could say anything, Chrissy ran down the hallway and Keisha chased her. After taking a few steps, Keisha turned around and pointed at Steve.

"If you got any sense, you better leave his ass alone Laura. He gon' do you the same way!"

She continued chasing Chrissy. After getting outside, she saw Chrissy leaned up against her car.

"It's okay girl. At least you know where you stand with him. I told you he was no good," Keisha said, rubbing her back. Chrissy fell into Keisha's arms and her sobs turned into hysteric cries.

Chapter II

Bounce Back

The next few days, Chrissy stayed in bed. How could she let a six-year relationship between Steve and Laura get past her? She cried and slept days away, even calling off work. Although she knew there was a chance she could lose her job, she didn't care.

Keisha went into Chrissy's room to check on her.

"You okay Chrissy?" she asked. "Look you gotta bounce back from this. I get that you're hurt, but you can't let that fool have power over you like that! Get up, get back into the swing of things, call your job, and go to work tomorrow. Lord knows I can't cover your half of the rent!"

Chrissy lay in silence. After getting no response, Keisha shook her head and left.

What Keisha didn't know was this was Chrissy's second time getting cheated on.

Her relationship before Steve was abusive. He would push, choke, and slap Chrissy. Days would pass by without Chrissy hearing a word from him. Sadly enough, she knew he was out cheating because he didn't try to hide it. He would come home expecting a hot meal to be waiting on him. After two years, Chrissy found the strength to leave him.

It was then that her grandmother passed, which left her feeling hopeless. After a while, she met Steve. Thinking he was the one, she was blinded by the love she developed for him. She ignored the signs.

Chrissy knew Keisha was right. She knew she had to bounce back from her heartbreak. She called her job and spoke with her boss, begging for forgiveness. Blaming her absence on an urgent family matter, her boss reluctantly agreed to give her another chance.

Chrissy peeled herself from the bed and tried to live again. She went to the bathroom first. Showering, brushing her teeth, and combing her hair made her feel somewhat human again.

She came out of the room and asked Keisha if she was hungry.

"Damn girl. You look different with your hair combed. I almost didn't recognize you!" Keisha said, laughing.

"You want something to eat or not?"

"Yeah, hook me up some pancakes and sausage!"

After they were done eating, Chrissy cleaned up the apartment, hoping the chores would put her back in a working mood. She ironed her clothes for work the next day. After she finished everything she could think of, the girls chilled and watched TV.

As Keisha crunched on a bag of chips, she kept glancing at Chrissy out the corner of her eye. She would turn her attention back to the TV, and then glance at Chrissy again.

"Why do you keep staring at me?"

With her eyes fixated on Chrissy, she asked, "Where is your daddy? I've never heard you talk about him."

"Because there's nothing to talk about. What do you want me to say, Keisha?"

"Something. Anything. I just don't know anything about him."

"Me either Keisha! I met him once, when I was twelve. He took one look at me and told me I wasn't his kid! I don't know shit about my sperm donor and I wanna keep it that way!"

Chrissy fought back tears.

Keisha scooted closer to her.

"Sorry Chrissy. I didn't know."

Chrissy wiped her face and told Keisha not to worry about it. She explained that she always wanted to know her father. So meeting him was like a dream come true, until he told her he wasn't going to have anything to do with her. She couldn't understand how a man could look his child in the face and say something so hurtful. He'd left her mother and ran off with another woman and her child.

Chrissy knew nothing about how a man should treat a woman. She latched on to anything that felt like love, which is why her relationships didn't work. She knew she needed to learn to love herself first before allowing anyone else to come into her life.

The next day, Chrissy walked into work with a smile on her face. Although it wasn't genuine, she didn't want people asking her any questions. As usual, she spoke to her coworkers. She strolled to her desk, pretending she was ok.

Once she sat down, she began her calls for the day. When she pulled her calendar out, she saw a picture of her and Steve sticking out from her notebook. She balled it up and tossed it in the garbage can. In a daze, the ringing of her work phone startled her.

"Good afternoon. Stone Marketing. Chrissy speaking. How may I help you?"

"So how long you gon' be mad at me Chrissy?"

It was Steve. Chrissy knew she couldn't fall back into his bullshit, so she quickly slammed the phone down.

She grabbed her forehead, took a deep breath, and continued working. Although life was hard for her at the moment, Chrissy knew time would heal all wounds. She knew she had to keep pushing forward and forget about the life she had known with Steve. She caught her tears, before they began streaming down her cheeks, and continued her workday.

****

Keisha was about to hit the club and asked Chrissy if she wanted to come with her.

"Naw, I'm okay. Thanks though. Have fun and be safe."

"Chrissy, you gon' have to get out one day. Quit being a home body," Keisha said.

Keisha always knew the best spots to go. She was the social butterfly of the two. Chrissy was pretty laid back, a stay-at-home kind of girl. She didn't mind missing out on the club scene. After all, she was still trying to get over Steve. So staying home was no big deal to her. She was comfortable there. She was safe.

Chrissy knew that if she didn't clear her mind, she was going to fall into a huge state of depression. She began to think about conversations she used to have with her granny. When she was a little girl, her granny would tell her to draw whenever she was mad. Not understanding, she still complied. Taking granny's advice as an adult, she resorted back to what she felt was a stress reliever. Grabbing her headphones and notepad, Chrissy sketched.

****

Chrissy was still a bit emotional, but she was feeling better after five months. Every now and then, she would get teary-eyed thinking about Steve. She would often wonder if he had married Laura yet. She'd gained fifteen pounds in the past few months. When she would think about her past, she would eat. Most of her weight went to her stomach and thighs. She was self-conscious, but she knew she had to snap out of it and continue to love the skin she was in.

Although she was okay with her weight gain, she would still get a bit self-conscious when around other people. No man wanted a woman with a big belly anyway, not that she thought about it much.

Chrissy knew she hit the jackpot when she met Keisha because Keisha balanced her. No matter how much they disagreed, Keisha never turned her back on her. Even if Keisha didn't agree with Chrissy's decisions, she always supported her.

As usual, Keisha was preparing for a night on the town. Surprisingly enough, Chrissy decided to join her. After being in the house for five months straight, she knew it was time to get out and enjoy herself.

"Come on girl before we be late!" said Keisha.

"Okay, okay!" Chrissy yelled. She coached herself, "These past five months don't matter. His loss, not yours. Make today count."

Chrissy's phone rang. It was her mom. As her mother went on and on about a wonderful guy she had been dating, it made Chrissy a bit sad. She wished to have the type of relationship with a guy that her mom had.

"That's great Mama, but I gotta call you back."

Chrissy caught the tears before they began to trickle down her face and started preparing for the night.

She put on her fitted, ripped jeans and sequence blouse. She grabbed her Red Bottom heels and slipped them on her freshly pedicured feet. Chrissy picked up her Mac lipstick and glided it across her full lips, and sprayed a dab of her Christian Dior perfume on both sides of her neck. She was ready.

Chrissy stepped out the room and signaled for Keisha so they could go.

"Damn bitch! Okay I see you! You trying to get picked tonight huh? It's about time. You need to move on."

"I guess," Chrissy replied.

Keisha and Chrissy got to the bar and it was popping. Music was on point and the crowd was decent. The girls found their way to seats by the bar. Keisha ordered two tequila shots. It had been a minute since Chrissy had any alcohol, so she knew to be careful.

As the hours went by, Chrissy warmed up more and more. Keisha was happy to see her best friend out enjoying herself instead of being cooped up in their apartment. She ordered another round of shots for her and Chrissy.

Yelling over the music, Chrissy told her, "Naw girl. One of us has to be able to drive back home. Ill just sip on this apple margarita."

"That's why I love you Chrissy!" Keisha hugged her best friend. "What would I do without you?"

She kissed Chrissy on her cheek and drunkenly swayed back and forth with her. Keisha got up and started dancing by her seat.

"Yes!! This is my jam!"

Chrissy shook her head at her best friend. As crazy as she was, Chrissy couldn't help but love her.

Keisha looked across the bar and spotted an old friend of the family.

"Chrissy I'll be right back!" Keisha yelled.

As Keisha danced her way over to her old friend, Chrissy stayed at the bar sipping on her apple margarita. As she bobbed her head to the music, a man sat next to her.

"Hello beautiful. How you doing? I'm Keith."

With reservation, Chrissy extended her hand to him.

"I'm Chrissy."

"You here by yourself?"

Pointing to Keisha across the room, Chrissy told him, "Nope. With her over there."

Keith laughed. "She must really be enjoying herself."

"Mmhm," Chrissy mumbled.

Keith kept trying to strike up a conversation with Chrissy only to run into dead ends.

"Why you so quiet?" he asked. "You seem a bit uptight."

Chrissy slowly turned her head in his direction.

"I'm usually not that talkative to someone I just met. I don't know you like that."

Keith looked at her and smiled.

"We can change that."

Surprisingly, they had much in common. Chrissy learned that Keith had just ended an unhappy relationship he'd been trying to get out of. She explained her breakup with Steve that happened months ago.

Keisha walked over to Chrissy and noticed she was talking to Keith.

"And who is this Chrissy?" she asked.

"Keisha this is Keith. Keith, this is my best friend Keisha."

Keisha shook his hand. "Nice to meet you Keith. You trying to holler at my girl?"

"Girl stop! We just talking," Chrissy chuckled.

"I mean, I would like to take her out if she would let me," Keith responded.

Chrissy stopped laughing and looked at Keith. She smiled and put her head down, embarrassed because she was blushing.

"Okay! Well y'all wrap up y'all lil conversation. We about to bounce Chrissy. I'll be over there by the door!"

Chrissy looked at Keith and smiled.

"Well," she said. "It was nice meeting you Keith."

She got up to walk away and Keith grabbed her by the hand. Chills went up and down her spine. It had been a minute since a man had touched Chrissy.

"What?" she asked him.

He insisted that they exchange numbers and keep in touch. Chrissy agreed.

****

Although she was still skeptical, Keith made her feel alive again. He surprised her with flowers at her job and love notes on her car. She couldn't deny how good it felt to be catered to after all she had gone through in her past relationships. He never pushed the issue of sex, always telling her that he would be more than willing to wait.

Keisha had been unemployed for about three weeks, but finally landed a job. She ran into Chrissy's room to share the good news.

"I got it, Chrissy! I got the damn job! Go me!"

Chrissy was ecstatic for her. They hugged and rejoiced.

"Wanna go out with me later to celebrate?" Keisha asked.

"No, thank you. Keith has a surprise planned for me. So he's coming to get me around nine-ish."

"Excuse me, heffa! But, for real, that's good. I'm glad he makes you happy. Plus, I haven't seen any bad signs, so he just may be a keeper for you!"

"Whatever girl!" Chrissy laughed. "Go ahead and enjoy yourself. I'll get with you later."

Keisha got dressed and headed out to meet up with some friends. Chrissy prepared for her night with her beau.

Once Keith was outside, he called for Chrissy to come down. She got to the car, and he waited with a dozen red roses. He opened the passenger door, kissed her on the cheek, and held her hand as she sat in the car.

"Chrissy, baby, you look stunning tonight."

"Thank you, Keith. You don't look so bad yourself," she said with a smile. "So where we headed?"

"Uh-uh babe. It's a surprise."

Chrissy nodded her head and sat patiently as he drove to their secret destination.

Upon arrival, Chrissy couldn't help but notice her name flashing across the billboard in front of the building, reading, "Chrissy, tonight belongs to you."

"Aw, Keith you did that for me? That's so sweet."

Keith kissed her on the cheek and got out of the car. He opened Chrissy's door and offered his arm to her. She smiled, wrapped her arm around his, and they headed inside.

He surprised her with a dinner date at the finest hotel. Music played in the background as they enjoyed a four-course meal, followed by a glass of Dom Perignon. Keith escorted Chrissy to the dance floor, and they held one another, gracefully gliding.

Just when she thought the night was over, Keith blindfolded her and led her to another room in the hotel. Once there, he revealed a huge, mirrored room full of rose petals. He directed her to the restroom where she put on a two-piece bikini he bought for her. After changing into her swimsuit, he led her to a Jacuzzi located across the room. He got in, and then helped her down the slippery steps. Once they were sitting down, relaxing in the bubbles, Keith began to give Chrissy a shoulder massage. As he rubbed her, he kissed her. Chrissy rolled her neck around so that Keith was sure to kiss every part of it. He turned her around and kissed her passionately. Chrissy pulled back. She stepped out of the Jacuzzi and signaled for him to do the same.

They went to the plush, circle bed covered with velvet sheets and rose petals as well.

Keith played some Luther Vandross. He laid her down on the soft bed and caressed her like never before. Untying her bikini top, he rubbed his fingertips across her erect nipples. Chrissy let out a slight moan. Keith turned her over and removed the rest of her bikini. He slowly kissed her from head to toe, and slid his manhood into her wetness. Chrissy moaned again, grabbing at the bed sheets. He threw her on top of him and she rode his long, thick slong. Grabbing at her breasts with one hand, and squeezing her ass with another, together, they let out a huge moan as they climaxed.

Chrissy rolled off Keith and lay next to him. He held her close to him and kissed her forehead. Closing her eyes and taking it all in, Chrissy couldn't help but smile. For the first time in a long time, she felt special. She felt like Keith could convincingly be the one.

As the night came to an end, she told Keith how much she would miss him, as he was going out of town on business. He promised her it wouldn't be long before they were together again. Keith dropped Chrissy off at home, and went on his way.

Chrissy went into her apartment and threw her keys on the table, waking Keisha up.

"Um, a little respect please?" Keisha mumbled. "Some of us are trying to sleep."

"Girl Keisha I'm sorry. I didn't know you were on the couch. Why aren't you in your bed?"

Keisha raised her head. With one quick look, Chrissy could tell that her friend was drunk.

"Ugh girl. Lay back down! Sleep that off!"

Keisha said, "No Chrissy. I wanna hear about your night. What was the surprise?"

Chrissy plopped down on the couch beside Keisha and began bragging about her night. As she spoke of Keith, she smiled. She told Keisha about the wonderful dinner, and how she and Keith danced with one another.

"He's the one Keisha girl. I'm telling you. I can feel it. You happy for me?"

After getting no reply, she looked at Keisha only to find her knocked out. Chrissy shook her head and smiled. She covered her best friend with a blanket and went to her room.

Grabbing her phone, she texted her man one last time for the night.

"Good-night Keith honey. I miss you and I can't wait to be in your arms again baby. Love you."

Chrissy closed her eyes and went to sleep.

Chapter III

Say What?

Chrissy was in a fantastic mood. Keisha, on the other hand, was still slumped against the cushions of the couch trying to recover from her celebration last night. Walking out of her room and seeing her best friend still drunk, Chrissy decided to wake her up. She went to the kitchen and got a tall glass of water. Tip-toeing to the couch, she slowly poured the water over Keisha's head.

"What the fuck are you doing?"

Laughing hysterically, Chrissy said, "Well how else was I gonna get you up?"

"Uh, like a normal damn person. Tap me!"

"Alright, sorry!" Chrissy apologized. "But it's time for you to get up. It's Saturday and we got shit to do."

"And what shit do we have to do?" she asked.

"Work out! We about to hit up Planet Fitness and burn some fat girl!" Chrissy exclaimed.

"Nope," Keisha told her. "You on yo' own with that. I'm about to lay back down."

As quick as Keisha laid her head back down, Chrissy snatched her up from the couch. Knowing she wasn't going to be left alone, she gave in to Chrissy's demands. She freshened up and the girls headed to the gym.

Once there, the girls checked in and hit the treadmill. While Keisha struggled, she noticed her friend was walking on the machine with ease, smiling the whole time.

"And what's gotten into you chick?"

"Nothing! Why you say that?"

Keisha gave her the side eye. "Really Chrissy? You woke me up at seven in the morning to come to Planet Fitness. You sang the whole way here. And you over there doing the treadmill like you used to it. So what's up?"

Chrissy looked at Keisha and grinned. She slowed her treadmill down. "Girl I had a great time last night. The shit was so dope! The hotel, the room, the sex, just everything was on point! Keisha, I think I love Keith."

"Okay okay! That's what's up! So the sex was banging?"

"Banging?" Chrissy asked. "That's an understatement! And girl the way he went down on me? Bitch that tongue is golden!"

"What? For real? Girl he sounds like a keeper!"

The girls continued talking as they walked the treadmill. They hit up a few more exercise machines and left. Before stopping home, they grabbed an avocado smoothie.

"Chrissy this shit is nasty! I can't drink this!" Keisha said.

"If you wanna lose that belly, then drink it."

Keisha took one last look at her smoothie before she downed it. She wiped the residue from her mouth and plopped down on the couch.

"So Chrissy, when is Keith supposed to be back?"

Chrissy took her toothbrush out of her mouth and spoke through the toothpaste filling her tongue. "He's coming back next Saturday. So I gotta be without my baby for a whole week."

"Girl hush." Keisha told her. "You will be alright."

Chrissy wiped her mouth and rinsed it out. Then she joined Keisha on the couch.

"I'm supposed to go to my mom's house tomorrow or so...something about her wanting to spend time with me and to meet some dude she's been seeing," Chrissy told Keisha.

"Aw that's cool. Mama getting her groove on too I see!" Keisha laughed.

"Girl I guess! But Mama got to have a life too huh?"

The girls decided to chill for the next couple of hours. It was then that Keisha came up with the idea of them having a few friends over to play board games and eat tacos. Chrissy had no objections. After all, she just wanted to pass time as best as she could since she couldn't spend any of it with Keith.

As the night approached, the girls had just finished preparing for their gathering. A few of Chrissy's coworkers, as well as some of Keisha's clubbing partners, stopped by. Twister, Guesstures, and Spades were the games of the night. Drinks were on deck, tacos arranged on single serving platters, and they all enjoyed themselves.

****

Chrissy woke up to find half of their company sprawled across their couch and living room floor. She slowly rose to her feet, waking up each person one by one. After seeing them to the door, she turned around and looked at how horrific their apartment was.

"Keisha. Get up. Girl, look at this damn mess we gotta clean up."

Keisha lifted her head and looked in disgust. "Chrissy, can we please do that shit later? I'm not trying to be cleaning up at 7:42 a.m on a damn Sunday."

Chrissy stomped her foot. "You think I want to? Hell, it was yo' brilliant ass idea to have company over."

"Chrissy girl don't act like you wasn't down, too!"

Keisha got up and started cleaning. "I'll take the kitchen and the bathroom. You get the living room and dining room?"

Chrissy agreed.

After the apartment was clean, Keisha showered and headed to the nail shop. She told Chrissy she would see her later.

"Okay, Keisha see you later."

Chrissy toasted a bagel. As she began to spread her favorite strawberry cream cheese on it, her phone rang. She felt giddy seeing Keith's name on the screen. She tossed the butter knife aside and answered.

"Hey Keith baby! I miss you so much! How's everything going?"

"I miss you too, my love. And everything is going okay. I just wish I could be home with you. But it won't be long...just a few more days."

"But I thought you had to be gone for a week?"

"Yeah it was supposed to be, but they changed it." Keith said. "I got more work put on me because I get to leave earlier. But it's okay. Thursday will be here before we know it, Chrissy."

Chrissy pouted. "Ok baby, as long as you thinking about me."

She sat down at the living room table and talked to Keith for fifteen minutes. He ended their conversation when he got a call from his boss.

Holding the phone close to her chest, Chrissy began counting the days away. "Monday, Tuesday, and Wednesday. Then I get to see my handsome baby."

Chrissy took a bite out of her bagel, frowning at how cold it had gotten. She heated it up and finished it.

Before she realized it, a few hours had gone by. Chrissy looked at the time and sighed. Keisha had just returned home from the nail shop.

"Girl ain't my nails pretty! Ming Lee be doing her thang!" Keisha waved her hands in front of Chrissy's face.

Seeing how Chrissy was in a bit of a daze, she asked her, "Girl why you looking all crazy?"

Chrissy looked up. "I really don't feel like going to Mama's house. I mean, I know she misses me and all that. And I know she wants me to meet her boyfriend or whatever. I'm just not in the mood. She's gonna be all caked up with her guy while I'm missing mine. I can't wait until Thursday gets here."

Keisha smacked her lips. "Really, Chrissy? You need to cut it out. Yo' man will be back in a few days. Besides, you always telling me how your mom deserves to be happy. So go be happy with her. Plus, if it makes you feel better, I'll go with you. I ain't got nothing to do anyway."

"Cool. I appreciate you Keisha. You my girl."

"Yeah yeah, whatever."

On the way, Chrissy called Keith. Although she had just spoken to him earlier, she couldn't help herself.

As they pulled up, Chrissy ended her conversation with him and the girls walked inside.

Chrissy's mom wrapped her in her arms, squeezing her before Chrissy could say hi.

"Baby! How you been? I missed you!"

"Hey Mama. I missed you too! How's everything?"

"Hey Ms. Smith!" Keisha said. "Looking good! Somebody got you glowing, I heard?"

Ms. Smith chuckled. "You heard, huh? Yes, Keisha darling. I gotta admit. I'm happier than I've ever been. It's been a long time coming."

The three of them sat down at the dinner table. Chrissy's mom talked about how wonderful of a man she was dating. As the girls asked questions, she happily answered. The doorbell rang.

"I'll get it girls!" Ms. Smith said with delight.

Keisha and Chrissy continued to eat and talk.

Chrissy's mom said, "Girls, I would like you to meet my baby."

Keisha looked up and instantly spit her food out.

Chrissy glared at her before she turned around, and her mom said, "Chrissy, meet Keith."

****

Keith and Chrissy locked eyes. They couldn't do anything but speak to one another.

"Hi. Hi, nice to meet you, Chrissy," Keith said, his voice slow.

"Likewise. Look excuse me, I don't feel so good." Chrissy wiped her mouth, got up from the table, and headed for the bathroom. Once reaching it, she slammed the door behind her. Feeling nauseous, Chrissy dropped to her knees in front of the toilet, and began to puke.

Keith stood next to Chrissy's mother as they held hands. Keisha slowly put her fork down and folded her arms. After hearing Chrissy from the dining room, her mom decided to check on her.

"Excuse me, baby, let me go check on my daughter."

She kissed Keith and headed to the bathroom. Keisha jumped up and said, "Um, I'll do it. Go'n enjoy your company."

After looking at Keith in disgust, Keisha headed Chrissy's way. She opened the bathroom door and entered, closing the door quickly behind her. "Chrissy, boo, you okay? Because, if you want, I can go snap on that bastard right now! In fact, let's do that!"

Keisha pulled Chrissy up from the floor and stormed toward the bathroom door.

"Wait...wait," Chrissy groaned, wiping her mouth with a towel. "I can't say nothing because it would kill my mama."

"But what about you, girl?" Keisha whispered.

"She's been through too much, Keisha, and you know it. Shit, you were just getting on me about being happy for her," she mumbled.

Keisha smacked her lips. "I know friend, but."

"But nothing Keisha. I can't say nothing. It would kill my mama."

Keisha extended her hand to Chrissy, helping her off the floor. She wiped the puke from her best friend's chin, and the girls headed back to the dinner table to continue with the night.

"You okay, baby?" Ms. Smith asked.

"Yeah, Mama. I'm okay." Chrissy cleared her throat.

"Good! Got me all worried about you, girl. But as I was saying, this is my handsome baby, Keith."

As Chrissy's mom doted on Keith, and all of his accomplishments, Chrissy's fury grew more intense. The more her mom spoke of Keith, the faster Chrissy tapped her foot against the floor. Keisha reached up under the table and put her hand on Chrissy's knee, signaling for her to stop.

Ms. Smith looked at Chrissy as she rubbed Keith's back. "So Chrissy, what you think about Keith? Nice fit for your old mom huh?"

"Uh, yea, okay. Mama I'm gonna let you two enjoy your night. Keisha and I are gonna head out." Chrissy rose from the table. "See you later, okay?"

The girls hugged Ms. Smith and they left.

Chrissy cried the whole ride home.

"It's gonna be okay. I promise it is," Keisha assured her.

When the girls got home, Chrissy's phone rang. It was Keith.

Keisha yelled out, "Bitch you better not answer that damn phone. Fuck him!"

Chrissy answered anyway.

"And what the fuck do you want? It ain't shit we need to talk about, so don't bring yo' sorry ass over here!"

She threw her phone on the bed, buried her head in her pillow, and cried some more.

A few hours later, she heard a knock on the apartment door. Chrissy got up and looked into the peephole. It was Keith. Weak for him and desperate for answers, she let him in. The more he apologized, the more vulnerable she became for him.

He made his way into her room. Chrissy pulled away from Keith as he pulled her toward him.

Not wanting to wake Keisha up, Chrissy whispered, "No, Keith. How could you do this to me? How could you lie to me?"

Keith put his finger on her lips and gently kissed her neck. He took his left hand and palmed the back of her thigh.

"No." She pushed him, but he came back.

"Yes."

Soon, she was naked. He turned Chrissy around, thrusting himself in and out of her. She knew she fucked up the moment she let him in, but she couldn't help herself. This dude had her stuck.

As he stroked her, she buried her head in her pillow, moaning quietly. Once Keith climaxed, he got up and pulled up his pants. He kissed Chrissy and left.

While putting the chain on the door, Chrissy bowed her head. She could not believe she was fucking the same dude as her mother. Sad thing was, she was not about to stop. She loved him too much.

Chapter IV

Can't Let Go

Chrissy tried to live life as she knew it before the incident at her mom's house. Keisha reminded her to keep her head up and stay strong.

"Chrissy, girl, neither one of us saw that coming. Don't constantly blame yourself. You didn't know. Mistakes happen. Just forget about him."

"It's easy for you to say that, Keisha," Chrissy uttered. "You ain't got no man, and ain't had a real relationship in years."

Keisha slammed her hand on the countertop and gave Chrissy a nasty look.

"For your information Miss Chrissy, I don't want no damn man. But I could have one if I wanted to, so don't get it twisted!"

"Sorry girl," Chrissy said. "You know I didn't mean it like that."

Walking to her with a cup of orange juice, Keisha said, "Yeah, yeah I know. Here, take this juice."

Chrissy sipped on it, then sat the cup on the end table and put her head down. She could not understand the betrayal. She started to doubt if it was even meant for her to be in a successful relationship.

"You don't need no man who can't appreciate you for the queen you are. Just forget about what you had with Keith and focus on yourself. True love will find you."

"Yeah, girl, you right," Chrissy said.

"I know I'm right. Besides, you are better off not talking to Keith's lying ass anyway. You know?"

Chrissy looked at Keisha and put her head down.

"Wait. Girl don't tell me you still been talking to him."

Chrissy didn't respond.

Keisha stood up from the couch. "Girl, you still been dealing with his lying ass? You crazy as hell! But hey, that's your decision."

Chrissy knew her best friend was right. But she also didn't care. She knew her mom was happy with Keith, but she wasn't about to cut him off because of that. When Keith would be with her mother, Chrissy would patiently wait her turn. Although Keisha called her all types of dumb bitches, Chrissy didn't pay her insults any attention because she was in love. After all, Keith promised to marry her just as soon as he could break it off with her mom. She figured that, soon enough, the chaotic situation would eventually work itself out. That way, Keith would be dedicated to her and only her. She had no doubt that she would be happier, in due time.

****

Chrissy and Keith carried on as if Chrissy's mother wasn't a factor. They spent time together whenever he wasn't at work or with her mom. When he would go to her mother's house, she was sure not to call his phone. In fact, she had grown so accustomed to sharing him, she hardly thought about it. Keisha, however, was sure to remind her.

"So, when all y'all gon' go on a date? Huh? And maybe afterward, y'all can have one big orgy. How about that?"

"Keisha, shut up. You ain't gotta be like that!"

"You don't either," she responded. "But hey, it's whatever." Keisha walked off.

Chrissy stood up. "Keisha, what's your problem with me?"

"Are you really asking me that, girl? Are you? You settled for a man who is fucking yo' mama! You act like you need a man around you to be complete. Get a damn backbone and value yourself!"

"Keisha, I love him!" Chrissy cried out. "What am I supposed to do?"

Keisha walked to her and sat her down. "Look. I'm not trying to judge you or tell you how to live your life. I just love you like a sister, and want the best for you. Regardless, you know I got yo' back. But don't expect me to be cool with Keith!"

Chrissy chuckled and hugged her friend, thanking her for always being there.

"So," Keisha said. "What are your plans for the day?"

The girls had a small conversation before going their separate ways for the day.

As Chrissy drove to the hair salon, all she could think about was the bittersweet life she was living. Loving a man who was having sex with her mother was not the relationship she imagined she would be in. But she could not bring herself to kick Keith to the curb. She thought about all the reasons things would work out in her favor.

"I'm young, pretty, and smart. I have a good job and I have potential. I can still have kids. Sure, my mom is pretty, too, but she can't hold his attention the way that I can. He's gonna pick me. I'm not worried."

She arrived at her hair salon and sat in her beautician's chair to get her ends trimmed. Ms. Rere always kept Chrissy's hair looking fly.

"Hey Chrissy!" Ms. Rere said. "What you been up to?"

Chrissy smiled. "Girl, nothing. Just working and being in love...the usual."

"Whoa! Don't try to skim past that love word! Who got yo' nose wide open?"

Chrissy didn't feel like explaining her situation. She wasn't the best liar, so people could usually see right through her. She quickly changed the subject.

"Ms. Rere, girl, you don't know him. But listen. I was thinking about changing up my look. I'm thinking I want a short hairdo. Chop it off."

Ms. Rere stopped clipping Chrissy's ends and quickly spun the chair around. "You sure? Your hair is past your shoulders Chrissy. How short are you trying to go?"

"I trust you. Do what you do."

Ms. Rere shrugged her shoulders. She turned the chair back around and went to work.

Once she was done, she gave Chrissy a mirror to look at it.

"I love it!" Chrissy yelled. "And you gave me highlights, too? Can't nobody tell me shit! Thanks Ms. Rere!"

"You are so welcome," Ms. Rere told her. "Thanks for always trusting me. Come back in a couple of weeks so I can give you a hot oil treatment. And take care of those highlights so your hair won't fall out."

"Will do. See you in two weeks!" Chrissy said as she walked out the door.

She knew she looked nice. She hoped Keith would feel the same about her slight transformation. She called him, but he didn't answer. Chrissy thought nothing of it.

Stopping at the corner store, Chrissy succumbed to a sudden craving for strawberry ice cream. When she walked in, two guys by the cash register complimented her. One tried asking her for her phone number.

"Thanks, but no thanks. I don't think my guy would want me to go out with another man."

"Okay, sweetie, no problem," the man said. "I ain't mad at you. You'll wish you gave me the chance later."

He smiled as left the store with the other one. As they got into a Mercedes Benz and drove off, Chrissy couldn't help but wonder if she made the wrong decision by not giving him a chance. But the thought quickly passed. Keith was her future.

When Chrissy made it home, she found Keisha on the couch.

"Hey Keisha. Where you end up going?"

Keisha looked up, her eyes wide open.

"Chrissy! Girl that cut is dope! But why did you cut off all that pretty hair?"

Smiling, Chrissy said, "Just wanted something new. Do you really like it Keisha?"

"Naw. I love it!"

****

When Chrissy walked in to work, all heads turned. Her coworkers complimented her on her new look. She thanked them and headed to her desk. Once she sat down, she looked in her desk mirror and smiled. It had been a while since she received so many compliments back to back, and it felt good. The text notification on her phone made her jump.

"Hey Chrissy love. I miss you. Let's do lunch today. 12:00? Our spot?"

She quickly accepted. She could not wait. She tried keeping herself busy until then. She filed paperwork, answered all calls, attended a brief meeting, and volunteered to fax papers for her coworkers. After looking at her watch and seeing that it was only 11:30 a.m, Chrissy sighed. She had finished all her work for the morning, so she could do nothing but wait.

****

Chrissy waited in the parking lot of Lawrence's Fish and Shrimp. When Keith pulled in, she hopped out of the car.

Jumping into his arms, she kissed him. "Hey, baby! I've missed you so much!"

Keith kissed her back. "I missed you too, love. Nice cut baby. Looks really good on you! But let's go eat. I only have forty-five minutes today. I gotta get back to this big meeting."

They ate quickly, talking between bites.

While heading back to their cars to go their separate ways, they held hands, but Chrissy's mood sank. She hated not seeing Keith as often as she wanted.

"Baby I really miss you," she said. "When can I see you?"

Keith brushed his hand across her cheek. "I promise I'll come over Saturday."

Chrissy nodded her head, kissed Keith, and they both headed back to work.

After her workday was over, Chrissy went home. She showered and lounged around, waiting for Keisha to get home from her new job. Bored, she thought about dinner. She made chicken breasts, topped with cheese, onions, and bacon, as well as a side of brown rice.

When Keisha got home, Chrissy started setting up the chicken. Keisha found her at the counter.

"Oh my God Chrissy. Thank you so much for cooking. I'm starving and tired as hell."

"No problem. But I wanna hear about your first day of work."

It was definitely a job she would have to get used to, but for now it would have to work. Keisha could not afford to not work. She knew that Chrissy could not pick up her slack anymore. As good as their conversation was, Keisha could not refrain from yawning every few minutes.

"Chrissy the food was good, and so was our little talk. But I'm beat, so I'm gonna go to bed now. Talk to you tomorrow."

Keisha went into her room and closed the door. Chrissy cleaned up behind the two, then went to sleep as well.

When Chrissy woke up the next day, she realized she had overslept. She hurried to make it to work on time, knowing it wouldn't be feasible.

After showering, she quickly got dressed and headed out. On the way to work, Chrissy felt somewhat nauseous and a bit lightheaded. She forgot to eat breakfast. Feeling the way she did, she knew she was in for a long Friday, so she stopped at the store and grabbed some Pepto Bismol.

Keisha had the day off, so she went to the store and bought dinner for the girls. Because she did not know how to cook like her best friend, she picked out a meal she was sure to not mess up: pre-made rotisserie chicken, mashed potatoes, and garlic bread.

Upon returning home, Keisha realized it was too early to begin preparing dinner, so she cut on the TV and watched Maury.

****

Chrissy came home and sat down on the couch next to Keisha. By then, dinner was prepared.

"What's wrong with you Chrissy?" she asked her.

Chrissy held her stomach. "I just don't feel so good. I think I need to eat or something."

"Perfect!" Keisha exclaimed. "Because I know you smell that good ass food I cooked for us!"

Keisha jumped up and grabbed their plates off the stove. She handed Chrissy hers and sat back down on the couch. Chrissy took the foil off the plate and looked at the food. She chuckled.

"What's so damn funny?" Keisha inquired.

"Nothing boo. But you know damn well you ain't cook this rotisserie chicken! I know they sell this at Food For Less!"

Keisha laughed. "So what? We eating, right?"

After the girls finished eating, Chrissy took their plates to the kitchen and washed them before she sat back on the couch with Keisha.

"So, what you doing tomorrow?" Keisha asked her.

"Well," Chrissy paused. "Keith and I are just gonna chill out. He said he misses me, so we're just gonna spend some time together."

"Oh okay. So where y'all going?"

Chrissy looked away. "Ah, we just gon chill out here," she muttered.

"Here?" What you mean y'all chilling out here? Sorry, but that's not about to happen!"

"Keisha come on now, don't start. You said you would respect my decision. I know you don't like Keith, but I love him. Besides, I live here too, you know?"

"Yeah whatever, I know." Keisha said. "You right. But just know that I'm chilling at home tomorrow too, but I'll stay out y'alls way."

Chrissy hugged her friend and they both went to bed.

The next day, Chrissy woke up and immediately texted Keith.

Although their relationship had been going on for quite some time now, Chrissy still liked Keith to see her looking her best. She brushed her teeth and gargled. While doing so, she got dizzy, so she hurried up and lay back down.

****

Chrissy had fallen asleep, so when he knocked on the door, Keisha had to answer.

"Who is it?" she asked.

Keith announced, "It's me, Keith."

Keisha flung the door open and walked away, demanding that he close and lock it behind him. She went back to her room and Keith entered Chrissy's room.

He nudged her to wake her up.

"Hey baby, how you feeling?" he asked her.

Chrissy rolled over and rubbed Keith's back. "I'm not feeling too good, baby. I guess that's why I drifted off."

"That sucks," he said. "What's wrong with you?"

"Not sure. I just started feeling this way yesterday morning, on my way to work. Must be something in the air. It's probably just a bug. I'm sure it'll go away."

Keith rubbed her cheek and insisted that she get some rest. Chrissy began to pout.

"Babe, you ain't gotta go."

"Naw, Chrissy, it's fine," Keith said. "Rest up. I got a run to make anyway. I'll be back later baby. I promise. And I'll stay the night with you."

Keisha went into Chrissy's room after Keith left. After Chrissy told her she had been nauseous for a couple of days, Keisha's eyes got big.

"Girl yo' ass is pregnant!"

"No, I'm not Keisha. Cut it out. It's just a bug. It'll go away."

"No! That ain't no bug!" Keisha proclaimed. "You about to have that fool's baby!"

Keisha left a little later, returning with a pregnancy test.

Meanwhile, Keith decided to visit his church. He needed to do a confessional.

"I need help, Father," he disclosed. "I don't know how to get myself out of this situation. I'm in love with someone I cannot be with. I'm trying to do what's right in the eyes of everyone else, but inside, I'm hurting and I need help."

Keith had begun crying to the priest.

The priest responded, saying, "I need you to do what is right in the eyes of God. You must choose, and choose wisely."

****

Chrissy still hadn't looked at the pregnancy test because she was afraid. She didn't bring it up when Keith got there, but she tried to act like nothing was on her mind when he crawled beside her in bed.

He finally fell asleep. Chrissy continued to watch TV and worry about the results of the test she left on the bathroom sink. Just then, the power went out. She couldn't find her phone, so she used the flashlight on Keith's phone instead. Without anything else to distract her, she gave in. She needed to know. She found her way to the bathroom, closed the door, and looked at the pregnancy test under the phone's light, glaring at the lines that told her Keisha was right.

Chrissy sat on the floor and smiled, as she held her stomach. She figured this was just what was needed for Keith to permanently break it off with her mom.

Keith's phone vibrated. Curious to see who could be texting him at 3:00 a.m, she opened it up.

"Baby, where are you? I'm waiting on you. I miss you."

Not recognizing the number in her man's phone, Chrissy snuck and called it.

A man answered, "Hello, baby."

Chrissy dropped the phone and screamed.

Chapter V

Three's Company

Her scream startled Keith. He jumped up and heard her panting in the bathroom, so he hurried to her.

"Baby what's wrong?"

Chrissy still gasped for air. Soon, all she could do was gasp, unable to get enough air into her lungs. She pushed Keith's hands away from her as he tried to pull her up from the floor.

As she slowly caught her breath, she rose from the floor and held on the sink for support.

"Baby what's the matter?"

"Get away from me!" Chrissy yelled. "Get the fuck away from me!"

She pushed Keith out of her way, ran to her room, grabbed her belongings, and quickly stormed out the door. As Keith prepared to leave out of the bathroom, he noticed the positive pregnancy test. He then picked up his phone and saw the number on the call screen.

"Shit!" he yelled.

Keisha opened her bedroom door. "What the fuck is going on?"

Keith stood silent. Keisha looked around and didn't see Chrissy. She walked up on Keith and stood toe to toe with him.

"Where the hell is Chrissy?"

With his head hung low, he mumbled, "She left."

"Well then nigga, you gotta leave too!"

Keisha followed Keith to the door with her arms folded and her mouth twisted. He could not get his heels out of the door before she slammed it on them. Then she went back to her room to call Chrissy. When Keisha dialed her, she heard Chrissy's phone vibrating underneath the couch.

"Damn, I gotta find her," Keisha uttered.

She put on her clothes and headed out to look for her best friend.

Chrissy drove to her mom's house as fast as she could. She cried the whole ride. Knowing this would break her mother's heart, she knew it was time to come clean. She couldn't do it anymore.

She reached her mom's house, jumped out the car, and ran to the front porch. Chrissy rang the bell frantically, but her mom didn't answer.

Chrissy plopped down on the porch and stared in silence. Just then, Keisha pulled up. She sprang out of the car and headed toward Chrissy.

"Chrissy, what's wrong? What happened?"

Chrissy slowly raised her head. "I'm pregnant by Keith."

"Um, okay boo. That's not too bad. We just gotta..."

"And he's gay, " Chrissy interrupted.

Keisha stopped mid-sentence and put her hand over her mouth.

"Bitch, what? Stop playing! So what the fuck are you gon' do Chrissy?"

"Imma take care of my baby."

"Okay, see now I'm finna get pissed the fuck off. Chrissy, how fucking stupid do you have to be to keep a baby with a gay nigga who's fucking yo' mama?"

"I don't expect you to understand, because I don't. I'm just following my heart."

She put her head on Keisha's chest and cried. Keisha hated the decision her friend was making. But now was not the time to scold her and turn her back on Chrissy. She held her in her arms and rocked back and forth with her.

"It's gonna be okay, friend. I swear to you it will," Keisha reassured her.

She picked her weeping friend up from the porch and walked her to the passenger side of the car. As Keisha drove home, Chrissy sobbed the whole time. Keisha couldn't help but feel sorry for her. Just when she thought she found the man of her dreams, Chrissy was heartbroken by his many infidelities. Keisha knew that she had to be Chrissy's backbone. And she was willing to do whatever it took to help her.

****

Chrissy hadn't mentioned Keith's name in a few weeks. Keisha had been noticing what appeared to be Chrissy moving on with her life. It was strange to her, but she didn't question it. She just wanted the old Chrissy back.

Chrissy had been a bit distant from her mother because she could no longer bring herself to tell her mom the ugly truth. She kept all phone conversations between the two of them at a minimum. Although Keith called and texted Chrissy numerous times within the past few weeks, she ignored his attempts. Even though she knew it would be hard, Chrissy understood that she would eventually have to face both Keith and her mother.

Because she wanted to clear her mind as often as possible, Chrissy joined a yoga class, as well as a Lamaze class. Most women in the class had their boyfriends and husbands to accompany them. So for Chrissy, the experience was bitter sweet. However, she adjusted as well as one would expect.

After getting home from her Saturday night yoga class, Chrissy started thinking about the future of her child. She was only three months pregnant, but she knew she had to put her feelings aside and develop a relationship with Keith for the sake of the baby. Even now, she was not over him. She hid the truth from Keisha and pushed Keith to the back of her mind for as long as she could.

Looking through all the texts from him, Chrissy finally decided to text Keith back.

"We need to talk. And not about us...about the baby."

She threw her phone down and went to shower. After drying off and putting on her pajamas, she noticed a response from Keith.

"Chrissy baby. I'm so sorry about all of this. I hate that you had to find out that way. I will make it up to you. Please let me. I love you."

Chrissy instantly felt confused. She knew that she wanted to give her child the life she didn't have; she wanted her child to have a relationship with the father, with both parents under the same roof. But she knew that she deserved better. She knew that any real man would be there for his child, whether he was with the child's mother or not. So she decided to stick to her original decision and stay single.

"Meet me at our spot tomorrow. 12:00 p.m."

****

When Chrissy showed up, Keith was already there. She slowly got out of the car. Keith walked over to her and tried to hug her, but Chrissy moved.

"Okay, you're right. I shouldn't have tried that."

"At least you got something right," she told him. "Look, let's go in and get this talk over with."

They headed inside, ordered food, and sat down.

"Look, Chrissy. I would be a fool to ask for a second chance. I know I don't deserve it. I just want to be there for you and my baby in any way that I possibly can."

"That's what I want, too, Keith," she replied. "We both know that nothing can ever happen between us again. But I refuse to keep your baby from you. And by the way, it would be a third chance, not a second."

"Thank you, Chrissy."

"Yeah," she responded.

Keith and Chrissy came up with a plan as to how everything would work between the two of them. After forty-five minutes had passed, Chrissy looked at the time on her phone.

"Shit! I gotta get out of here before I'm late to my class."

Keith wiped his mouth. "What class?"

"Lamaze," she said.

"Can I go?"

"Nah," Chrissy said, unsure of her response. "That's not a good idea."

"I just want to be there every step of the way. That's all. I wanna bond with my kid."

Chrissy looked at him. Although she hated what Keith had done to her, she figured it would be no harm in allowing him to join the class with her.

Upon reaching the Lamaze class, Chrissy headed in, with Keith following. Because she had attended the first two classes alone, everyone was somewhat surprised to see a man accompanying Chrissy this time.

The instructor said, "Okay class, let's get started. But before we do, we must always introduce newbies to the class. So, Chrissy, who is the nice gentleman you brought with you today?"

Chrissy hated that everyone's attention was on her. Again, since she was such a bad liar, she just introduced him as Keith. Although it would have been nice to introduce him as her significant other, she knew she shouldn't.

"Okay...well welcome to the class, Keith! You two have a seat. We were just getting started."

Keith and Chrissy sat down. The class started off with the usual breathing techniques. It was then time for the men to get behind the women to support them during the labor technique being practiced. To Chrissy's surprise, the instructor had called on her and Keith to lead the exercise.

Keith slowly sat behind Chrissy and began to pull her back toward him. Uneasy, but not showing it, Chrissy scooted back to him. As the teacher instructed all of the men to reach around and rub the bellies of the mothers, Keith did just that.

The technique was one that the mothers enjoyed. It was comforting for them to be able to relax and be catered to. Chrissy had been pretending, for the last thirty minutes, that she and Keith were okay. When it was time for the men to help the mothers to their feet, Keith stood up and extended his hand to Chrissy. She grabbed it and he helped her up. As soon as she was on her feet, Keith rubbed his hand across Chrissy's cheek as he always did.

It reminded her of when they were happy. He kept his hand on her cheek and she stood there, staring into his eyes. The chemistry between the two of them was so intense at that moment that the instructor had to call Chrissy's name.

"Chrissy? You doing okay?" she asked.

"Uh, yea. Yea I'm ok," Chrissy answered as she pulled Keith's hand from her cheek.

As the last fifteen minutes of class continued, Chrissy couldn't deny the fact that she was having a great time. While she always enjoyed it, she never truly was able to walk away from Lamaze class with a smile on her face.

"Okay guys," the instructor said. "Everyone did great today. And let's give Chrissy and Keith a round of applause for leading today's labor technique!"

As the class clapped for them, Keith and Chrissy smiled. They thanked everyone for their kind words, and everyone left.

Once Chrissy got to her car, she proceeded to open the door but Keith stopped her, grabbing her arm and gently turning her toward him.

"Look Chrissy. I know you love me. And I love you just the same. I want you and I know you want me."

Chrissy slowly pulled her arm back. "Keith, it doesn't matter what I want because if it did, you would be with me, and not some damn man and my mama!"

"I'll cut it off with dude," he pleaded. "I swear. Just take me back."

Chrissy absolutely could not believe she was even considering Keith's offer. She knew she had no business dealing with him on an intimate level anymore, but her heart just wasn't ready to let go.

"And what about my mama?" she inquired. "You gon' break it off with her too?"

"Baby, you know that's a little more complicated. And it's gonna take a little more time. But yes, I'm willing to tell her when the time is right. I just don't wanna lose you Chrissy."

Chrissy couldn't grasp the words coming from Keith's mouth. What could he possibly mean when he said, "When the time is right?" She was pregnant with his child. What time could be better than now?

"Look, Keith. I'll think about it. I gotta go. Just meet me at class next week."

She got in her car and pulled off.

****

Chrissy hummed and smiled while ironing her work clothes. She would giggle every now and then. While prancing to the kitchen, Keisha's suspicious eyes stopped her.

"Uh, and why you so happy?" Keisha asked her.

Chrissy couldn't tell Keisha that Keith had come to class with her. She couldn't tell her Keith was still carrying on a relationship with a man, as well as her mama. And she knew she couldn't tell her that she was contemplating giving Keith a third chance.

"Huh? Oh no reason in particular. Just feeling good for a change. That's all!" Chrissy replied with a smile.

"Well, happy is always good in my book." Keisha told her. "But you need to rub some of that happiness off on me because I sure as hell could use it."

"Why, Keisha? What's wrong?"

"Girl, that damn job! I'm over it. Too much work, too little pay!"

"Yeah, I hear you, but you gotta do what you gotta do until you can find better," Chrissy shrugged. "But I'm about to go ahead and lay down. Do you wanna come to my mom's house with me tomorrow?"

"Why you gotta go there?"

Chrissy paused. "Uh, I think it's time for me to tell my mama that she's gonna be a grandma."

"You sure about this Chrissy?"

"Naw...naw I'm not actually. But shit, I can't hide it forever."

Keisha shrugged her shoulders and nodded. "Okay, I'm down."

"Cool. Okay, good night Keisha."

Chrissy sat on her bed, holding her stomach while thinking of Keith. She had so many mixed emotions about everything. But one thing she was certain of was that she still loved Keith. Without wanting to sound desperate, or like she was over what he did, she decided to send him a short text message.

"Good night Keith. See you soon."

Chrissy curled up underneath her covers and fell asleep.

****

After work, the girls met up and headed to Chrissy's mother's house. As they approached the door, Chrissy took a deep breath. After ringing the doorbell, she looked at Keisha with fear heavy in her eyes.

"Chrissy, you got this. You are grown. Yo' mama's opinion, good or bad, does not matter. Do what you wanna do. You been doing good, handling yo' business, and taking care of yourself. So stop worrying," Keisha said. "You ready now?"

Chrissy let out a sigh. She smiled and shook her hands at her sides. "Girl, what would I do without you?"

They hugged one another just as Chrissy's mom answered the door stepping aside so they could walk in.

"And what made y'all stop by?" Ms. Smith said. I'm happy to see y'all, though. Ain't nobody bothered to check on me for a few weeks now! Hell, Keith ain't even been around that much either! He pops in and out. But that's neither here nor there. Glad to see you girls. I've been needing to talk to you anyway, Chrissy."

Keisha and Chrissy couldn't avoid looking at each other. Chrissy's mom looked at them, her own suspicion plain on her wary eyes.

"Uh uh," Ms. Smith said. "What's up y'all? Talk to me."

"Ma," Chrissy replied. "I'm pregnant."

To their surprise, Chrissy's mother was overjoyed. She hugged Chrissy so tight that Chrissy had to push her off.

"I'm so happy, baby! Let's have a celebration! Invite your boyfriend over so I can meet him!"

"Um, he's out of town, but maybe next time Mama," Chrissy fibbed.

"Okay! Okay! Well sit down anyway. I'm gonna cook some tacos." She clapped her hands together as she turned toward the kitchen.

"Okay. But Mama, what did you wanna talk about?" Chrissy wondered.

Her mother turned around. "Uh baby, that can wait. Today is about you."

As Ms. Smith turned back around and headed toward the kitchen, her smile turned into a look of concern. She was sure to hide it from the girls, though.

Chrissy looked at Keisha and smiled.

"I can't believe she's taking it like this."

"Yeah that's dope right? Mama is about to be somebody's grandma, huh?"

The girls laughed.

"Whew! I gotta tell you though, Keisha...I feel good. I'm gonna take care of my baby and we gon' be all good!"

"Yes, boo, yes!" Keisha yelled.

As the girls laughed, Chrissy said, "Girl I gotta use the bathroom. I'll be back!"

As Chrissy made her way down the hall, all she could do was smile. As bad as it sounded, she was happy that her mom hadn't heard from or seen Keith as much. Chrissy figured that he was finally breaking it off with her mom, slowly but surely. Even though she hadn't told

Keisha about her and Keith possibly working on fixing things, she was still proud of herself. She felt like everything was falling into place.

She reached her mom's bathroom and closed the door. As she stood up to flush after peeing, she noticed a piece of paper that fell from the back of the toilet. She picked it up to put it back, but something caught her eye. The letter had the word "Confidential" on it. Chrissy peeled the letter open and began to read it.

"Dear Ms. Smith,

We tried reaching you by phone, per your request. Upon several failed attempts, we decided to send a letter of notification. We regret to inform you that you are HIV positive."

Chapter VI

It's Not My Fault

Chrissy stood in shock. She could not believe what she had just read. She ran to the front room with the letter in her hand.

"Mama! What's this? You HIV positive!"

Chrissy's mother slowly turned around from the stove and looked at Chrissy.

"Baby, I'm shocked, too. I'm sorry. I've been meaning to tell you for a few weeks now. But don't worry. I'm gonna be okay. The doctor said..."

"Don't worry?" Chrissy yelled. "Did Keith give you HIV? Tell me now!"

Ms. Smith walked to Chrissy and put her hand on Chrissy's shoulder.

"Baby, no. I was told I've had it for quite some time. I suspected it a few months back, but I didn't think my symptoms were a big deal."

Chrissy snatched her shoulder away. "So you gave it to Keith? How could you do this? How could you be so goddamn careless? You out here fucking him knowing something was wrong with you!"

Chrissy's mother didn't hide her shock. Her mouth hung open, her eyes blank.

"Chrissy. Why are you making this conversation about Keith?"

"Why are you not making this conversation about Keith? What am I supposed to do? What about me? What about my baby?" Chrissy screamed.

Keisha stood in silence. She was in complete disbelief. As much as she wanted to intervene, she knew she should stay out of it. The truth needed to come out.

"Your baby?" Ms. Smith asked. "I'm confused."

"Yes Mama! My baby! Keith is the father! We've been together just about as long as y'all have! I love him! And you just destroyed my future, his future, and our baby's future!"

Chrissy stormed out the door. Ms. Smith fell down onto the couch, her hands covering her mouth.

Keisha looked at Ms. Smith. "I'm so sorry, Ms. Smith. I don't know what to say."

Ms. Smith did not reply.

"Okay," Keisha said. "I guess I better go check on Chrissy."

Keisha closed the door behind her and left with Chrissy.

On the way home, Chrissy stared out of the car window. She had cried so much, that she couldn't bring herself to do so anymore. She was upset, but more concerned about her and her baby's future.

"You ok ay, Chrissy?"

"Would you be?"

"Look, I understand you have been through more bullshit than you care to talk about. But you shouldn't have talked to your mama like that. It's not her fault."

"Not her fault? Not her fault?" Chrissy responded. "She fucked my man, all while knowing something was wrong with her. How is it not her fault? You sound stupid as hell!"

"It's not her fault because she didn't know you and Keith were together! You knew they were together though! And yo' ass continued fucking him! So who's the stupid one Chrissy?" Keisha fired back.

"Whatever!" Chrissy yelled.

"Yea I know it's whatever! But I'll tell you what. You not about to be talking to me like you crazy because I've done nothing but be there for you! Even when you were making the most fucked up decisions, I had your back. So you can save all that tough talk because I'm not the one to take it out on! The only thing you need to be focused on is getting checked to see if you are HIV positive!"

Chrissy knew Keisha was right, but she wasn't willing to admit it at the moment. She continued staring out the window until they arrived home.

Once in her bedroom, Chrissy tried to figure out her next step. She called and made an emergency appointment with her doctor. She then wondered if Keith had known about her mom having HIV. Is that the reason why he hadn't been around Ms. Smith like he used to be? Did he pass it on to the man he had been fucking? Would the baby be okay? Many thoughts crowded Chrissy's head. She knew she should be resting for work tomorrow, but sleep was the last thing on her mind. Confronting Keith about the situation had to be done, and Chrissy was more than willing.

Chrissy picked up her phone and texted Keith.

"Hey, Keith. I need to talk to you. It's important. Meet me at Judy's Bar & Grill in thirty minutes."

****

Chrissy sat at the table and signaled for Keith to come to her.

"What's this about, Chrissy?"

"Did you know?" Chrissy asked, unwilling to make small talk. "Did you know about my mother having HIV??"

Keith sighed. "Chrissy, I found out a couple of weeks ago. I tried reaching out to you, but you ignored all of my texts and calls. What was I supposed to do?"

"You were supposed to find a way to tell me!" she shouted.

Patrons turned their heads toward her, so she settled back in her chair. As the waitress headed to their table, Keith held his hand up, signaling to her that everything was okay.

"Lower your voice, Chrissy," he demanded. "Okay, I get your frustration. I'm just as mad as you. But you wouldn't answer my calls! My hands were tied! It's not my fault!"

Chrissy took a deep breath.

"So now what?" she asked Keith.

"Now we get through this together. Have you seen the doctor yet? Have you gotten tested?"

"My appointment is tomorrow," she answered. "I'm not going to work. I'm gonna call off."

"Do you want me to go with you?"

Chrissy nodded.

"Okay, I'm there. I'll call off, too. But since we here, there's no need to waste a trip. I'll order us some food. I know you gotta be hungry."

After eating in silence, Keith walked Chrissy to her car and helped her in. She drove off into the night, with Keith not too far behind her.

Once Chrissy got home, she was sure to text Keith to let him know, per his request. She lay her head down and attempted to rest.

****

Chrissy got dressed and headed to her doctor's appointment. The whole ride there, she prayed for a miracle. She prayed to God that, somehow, she didn't get infected. Although she tried preparing herself for the worst, she was sure as hell hoping for the best.

Once she arrived, she saw that Keith was already in the parking lot waiting for her. In her twisted mind, Keith was the greatest for supporting her. After Chrissy checked in, she sat next to Keith in the waiting room. He held her close, and she rested her head on his shoulder. He rubbed her belly as they waited for her name to be called.

People around them smiled, and Chrissy forced a smile back. They had no idea the kind of life they lived. One lady even congratulated them on their new pregnancy and advised Chrissy to be grateful that Keith was as supportive as he was.

"Chrissy Smith?" the nurse called out.

Chrissy took a deep breath and they headed back.

Once in the room, the nurse took Chrissy's vitals. She asked what brought her in, noting her next appointment was three weeks away.

"Um, I need to get tested." Chrissy replied.

Seeing how reluctant Chrissy was in sharing her reason why, the nurse assured her everything would be okay, and that the doctor would be in shortly to talk to her.

****

Chrissy and Keith headed back to get the test results. As much as she had prayed for a positive outcome, she didn't get her wish. She, too, was HIV positive. The doctor explained that she would have to take medications throughout her pregnancy. He also told her what to expect after childbirth, as well as all of the testing the baby would go through. Most of the information barely broke through Chrissy's daze, but she felt a little relief when she heard him say there was a chance the baby wouldn't be infected.

After leaving the clinic, Keith asked Chrissy if she wanted to stay at his house for a few days. Chrissy agreed. She went home and gathered clothing for the next few days. She texted Keisha and told her she was going to stay with Keith for a few days and not to worry. At this point, Chrissy couldn't care less what Keisha thought about her being with Keith. She knew that her best friend would always be there for her, regardless.

When they arrived at Keith's house, Chrissy slowly walked in. She placed her bags on his couch and sat down. Keith straightened his bed and led Chrissy to his room so she could rest.

"Baby, I gotta run to the office for a second to tie up some loose ends with this contract. I'll be back in about an hour or so. But if you need me, don't hesitate to call me," he told her.

He kissed Chrissy's forehead and left. Once she knew he was gone, she began walking around his home. Like any scorned woman, she started looking for signs of someone else having been there. She looked in his bathroom, under his bed, and even checked his garbage. She found nothing.

"What am I doing?" she asked. "This man would be crazy to bring me here if he was still on bullshit. Let me sit my ass down and relax."

She grabbed a bag of chips and a bottle of water and went back to Keith's bedroom. As she lay there snacking, she thought about all the shit she had been through. But somehow, she was still happy that she ended up with Keith, even under the circumstances. Chrissy had begun to trick herself into thinking that her life with him was supposed to end up the way it had. Yes, she had HIV. Yes, Keith had it also. But finally, she had his undivided attention. And she was happy.

A couple hours passed, and Chrissy still hadn't heard from Keith. Trying not to think negatively, she picked up her phone to call him. Just as she did, he texted her letting her know he was on his way home. After letting out a sigh of relief, Chrissy got up and headed to the bathroom.

She stood in front of the mirror and stared at herself, the blur of the past months coming into focus on the distension in her abdomen. "I'm going to be a mommy." She smiled.

Chrissy turned on the faucet and let the water run into the palms of her hands while splashing it on her face. She stood up and began swaying her hands around, searching for a face towel, slightly blinded by the water in her eyes. Once she stumbled across one, she dried her face and placed the towel back on the tub. Before leaving the bathroom, she straightened the rugs, pulled the shower curtain closed, and closed Keith's medicine cabinet.

As she closed the cabinet, she noticed a slew of medications. For a second, Chrissy was brought back to reality. She knew that she, too, would have to do the same thing. Her cabinet would look a lot like his, which held multiple orange bottles with his name on them. But she quickly snapped out of it. She was too happy about how things had turned out for her and Keith. Nothing else mattered...not even HIV itself.

****

Keith finally made it home. He kissed Chrissy and headed to the living room to catch sports highlights on ESPN. After a few minutes, Chrissy sat next to him and the two continued watching TV. As a few minutes passed, Chrissy rested her head in Keith's lap and stretched her body out on the couch. Keith reached down and rubbed her belly in a circular motion. He then combed his fingers through her hair and gently kissed her forehead. Chrissy closed her eyes and took the moment in. She then reached up and gently rubbed her hand against Keith's zipper.

Keith tensed under her. Chrissy took the cue, sat up, and straddled him. She kissed his neck and unhurriedly brushed her lips across his cheek until she reached his lips. She stuck her tongue into Keith's mouth and kissed him. He caressed her breasts and she moaned. Keith got up and pulled his pants down. He turned her around and pushed himself inside of her wetness. The more he stroked her, the louder she moaned. She knew Keith was getting ready to cum because she could feel the tension building up in him.

"Yes!" she screamed out to him. "You feel so good, baby!"

Keith could no longer hold it. He released inside of Chrissy, letting out a scream of relief. Once he was done, he pulled out of her and slowly walked to the bathroom to clean her off him. Chrissy followed.

As the two cleaned themselves off, Chrissy smiled. It seemed as though Keith's sex had gotten even greater. Or could it be that Chrissy hadn't had it in a while? Either way, she was extremely pleased.

"Come on Keith baby. Let's go to bed," she insisted.

"Okay babe. I'll be there in a second. Go ahead, I'll meet you in there after a while."

He slapped Chrissy's booty as she walked toward the bedroom. After seeing her to the bed, Keith tucked her in, cut the light off, and pulled the door up behind him.

After about an hour or so, Chrissy woke up and noticed that Keith was still not in bed. She peeped out the bedroom door and noticed that he fell asleep on the couch. Not wanting to disturb his comfort, Chrissy placed a blanket on top of him. She kissed his cheek and headed back to bed.

****

Chrissy sat up in bed and stretched her arms, letting out a long yawn. She got up and decided to cook breakfast for her man. When she opened the bedroom door, she noticed that Keith was pouring orange juice in a glass. Next to the glass was breakfast that he already prepared: Toast, bacon, scrambled eggs, and fruit.

"Oh my goodness, babe, you did this for me?"

Keith led Chrissy to a chair. She sat down, and he scooted her chair closer to the table.

"Good morning, my love," Keith responded. "Let's enjoy breakfast. I have a special day planned for us."

"But I thought you had to work," she replied.

"Nope," he answered. "I'm all yours. So eat up. Once we're done, get dressed for the occasion."

"But I don't know what the occasion is, Keith baby."

"Just be sure to look your best."

Chrissy and Keith ate their breakfast. Once done, they showered together, put on their best attire, and headed out.

Chrissy was pleasantly surprised about the day Keith had set up for them. First, they went to an art museum, which Chrissy absolutely loved. Then they ate lunch at a fancy restaurant, followed by a surprise maternity photo shoot. The final event of the night was Chrissy's favorite, an old school 90's R&B concert with lots of Chrissy's favorite artists, followed by an astounding marriage proposal. Of course Chrissy accepted!

On the ride home, Chrissy couldn't stop staring at Keith.

"What Chrissy? Why are you looking at me like that?"

Chrissy smiled. "You make me so happy. I can't wait to be your wife."

He returned the smile and grabbed her hand, squeezing it during the rest of the drive.

Over the next couple of months, Chrissy couldn't have asked for a better life. She continued with her Lamaze and yoga classes, she kept up with her medications, and she was engaged to the man of her dreams. Although conversations with her mother were few, she still loved her and respected her. She often hung out with Keisha, too. Chrissy quit her job and stayed at home with Keith. Keith wanted no fiancée of his working while pregnant, so he picked up the slack.

Chrissy thanked God everyday for bringing Keith into her life. Although things were shaky with them for quite some time, Chrissy was ecstatic that she could finally rest easy, knowing Keith belonged to her and only her. She was the mother of his child and his soon-to-be wife. What could possibly go wrong at this point?

Chapter VII

Redrum

Chrissy felt every bit of her pregnancy. Although she only had one more month to go before her baby girl was due, she became more anxious by the day. Her ankles were nonexistent and her feet were twice their normal size. Keith would usually rub them for her, but since he was not home, Chrissy texted Keisha.

"Keisha, what's up girl? Don't you wanna do me a huge favor and come over to massage my feet? You'll be my girl for life!"

After getting no response for the next twenty minutes, Chrissy decided to try to massage her own feet. Just as she did, her phone rang.

Before Chrissy could say hello, Keisha started loud-talking her. "Girl hell naw I'm not about to come over there and rub yo' big ass swollen feet!"

Chrissy pulled the phone away from her ear and placed it on speakerphone.

"Okay, Keisha damn!"

"But what we can do is go to this massage parlor that just opened up down the street from my job."

"Cool! I'll be ready in an hour!"

Keisha picked her up, and once they reached the parlor, Chrissy became quiet. She had a look of fear on her face.

"What's wrong, girl?" Keisha asked.

"What if I'm not a good mother? What if I'm not a good wife? What if I fail at all of this?"

"Girl, hush," Keisha said. "You were born ready. You're the most responsible person I know. I may not like some of the decisions you make, but I have no doubt that baby Breanne will be well taken care of."

"So you like the name I came up with?"

"Breanne is a beautiful name. I'm gonna spoil my goddaughter so much!" Keisha yelled.

"Girl, calm down," Chrissy told her as she laughed. "Come on and let's get these massages. Lord knows I need it!"

As the girls relaxed into the beds while masseuses worked on their upper bodies, Keisha asked Chrissy where Keith was.

"Oh girl you know he's always working," Chrissy answered. "He should be home shortly after I get there."

"Cool," Keisha replied. "So, when was the last time you spoke to your mother?"

"A couple of weeks ago," Chrissy mumbled.

Keisha sat up and looked at the massage therapists. "Could you two give us a minute please?" she asked them.

Once they left the room, Keisha turned to Chrissy. "Friend, enough is enough. I know you are probably still mad at your mother, but she's not to blame. She deserves to have her granddaughter in her life. Give her that chance."

Chrissy slowly lifted herself from the massage table. "Keisha I know, I know. It's just that we are not as close as we used to be."

"Because you let Keith come between y'all. That's why!" Keisha exclaimed. "Look Chrissy, for as long as I've known you, you have always adored your mother. Hell, you used to put her needs before your own."

"And that's the problem Keisha! It's no longer about my mother. It's about me!"

"Calm down before you go into labor!" Keisha demanded. "I'm just saying. If something happened to your mother, you would lose your mind and you know it."

"Yeah maybe."

"Whatever. Look, I'm taking a small road trip this weekend. Wanna come with me? I'm sure you could use a two-day getaway."

"Yeah, ok girl."

****

As Keisha drove Chrissy home, she gave her all the details for their upcoming road trip. She also told Chrissy to be sure to get plenty of rest the night before.

"Ok Keisha I'll be ready. Thanks for the massage. I really appreciate you."

"No problem girly. See you in a couple of days!"

Chrissy walked into the house looking for Keith after noticing his car was outside. She found him in the shower.

"Hey, babe. Why you home so early?"

"Oh work was a bit light today! How was your day? Where did you go?"

"Keisha treated me to a massage," she answered. "I know you usually hook me up but I couldn't pass on that offer!"

Keith and Chrissy laughed. Once he got out of the shower, he ordered Chinese food.

"What you wanna watch babe?" he asked her.

"You pick," she replied. "It doesn't really matter."

"It don't matter because all you gon' do is fall asleep anyway!"

"Ha ha. Not funny, big head," Chrissy grinned. "Oh yeah, I'm gonna ride to Indiana this weekend with Keisha. She has something going on there and I told her I wouldn't mind going with her."

"Cool baby. No problem. I just want you to be safe on the road with my baby girl in your belly." He rubbed her stomach.

"I'll be careful. We will be back Sunday night."

Keith held Chrissy as she fell asleep. He finished the movie and went to sleep as well.

****

"You got everything, baby?" Keith asked Chrissy as she packed her bag for the weekend.

Grabbing her toothbrush, she yelled, "Yes babe! Keisha is outside waiting for me. I'm about to go. See you later!"

"Not without giving me my kiss first."

He ran over to Chrissy, grabbed her and gave her a big hug and kiss.

"Love you Keith. See you in a couple of days!"

Chrissy headed out. She signaled for Keisha to pop her trunk so she could put her bag in it. Once she plopped down in the passenger seat, Keisha asked her, "You ready?"

Chrissy gave her a thumbs up and the girls headed to Indiana.

"Keisha, I'm proud of you taking the necessary steps to start your own business. This expo should help you out a lot," Chrissy said.

"Thanks, girl," Keisha said. "I just can't be at this job my whole life. It's just a means to an end Chrissy."

Chrissy nodded in agreement.

As Keisha drove, all Chrissy could think about was Keith. No one could possibly understand why she stuck by his side, even after all his lies and infidelities. She had lost her exes to other women and she wasn't about to lose Keith, too. She knew he would come around, and he did just that. The only thing left to do was for them to walk down the aisle. And that was only three months away.

Once they reached the hotel, the girls got out and headed to their rooms. They freshened up and headed to the expo, which was due to start in a couple of hours.

****

"Keisha girl, I really enjoyed my mini vacation. Thanks again."

"No problem," Keisha said, smiling. I want you to be a part of everything I do when it comes to this new business venture. Besides, I need your help anyway."

"Cool," Chrissy said. "Hey, you think you could drop me off at my mom's house? I think I need to fix our relationship."

Keisha smiled. "No problem! Hell, you are gonna need her help anyway!"

"You right!" Chrissy laughed. "Anyway, I'm sure Keith will be pleasantly surprised to see me back a day early."

"I'm sure he will."

Keisha pulled up to Chrissy's mom's house. As Chrissy started to ring the doorbell, she noticed that the door was cracked. Before she questioned it, she walked in.

Once in, the girls heard slow jams blasting from the back of the house. Chrissy called out for her mom, but received no answer.

"Keisha, stay right here. I'll be right back," Chrissy demanded.

"Okay, girl. I'm about to raid her refrigerator anyway."

Keisha began rummaging through Ms. Smith's refrigerator as Chrissy made her way to her mom's room. Chrissy slowly pushed the door open, her eyes stopping at her mom above Keith, riding him like a champ. Keith caressed her breasts and Chrissy felt her stomach rise into her throat.

Chrissy went blank, unable to move or speak. Her mind felt empty, but she knew something was sprouting there. As she watched her mother throw her head back, she found herself moving, but she still couldn't form a proper thought. She looked on her mother's dresser, by the door, and grabbed a screwdriver. Chrissy walked to the side of the bed and stood there, firm and unsure of her next step. Keith turned as she pulled the screwdriver up, but before he could yell out, Chrissy brought the screwdriver down into her mother's back, blind rage pouring into her arms and out of her mouth.

"How could you?" Chrissy yelled.

Keith jumped up and grabbed Chrissy's hand, preventing a fourth stab. Keisha ran into the room, her voice shrill.

"Oh my God, Chrissy! What the fuck did you do?"

Keisha called 911 and tried to stop Ms. Smith's bleeding by compressing her stab wounds with a big bath towel. Keith let Chrissy go and she stood there, her eyes as stone as her thoughts. With blood splattered over her face, she watched as Keisha tried to save her mom's life. Keith backed away from her, grabbed his clothes, and ran out the door.

The police and paramedics finally arrived. As the EMT's performed CPR on Ms. Smith, Chrissy still watched, the screwdriver loosely in her grasp. The police asked Keisha what happened, and through tears, she gave up her best friend. She cried, but Chrissy barely heard her. They handcuffed Chrissy and put her in the squad car. Chrissy didn't breathe a word, only seeing her mother's body even after she was taken away from it.

****

Keisha headed to jail to visit Chrissy. She was so unsure of how to approach her. It almost stopped her from going.

After patiently waiting, she was finally able to see her. As she picked up the phone to talk to her, she noticed how grimy the glass window was, and thought about how badly Chrissy would normally want to clean it.

When she realized Chrissy had come in, she waited until Chrissy picked up the phone, tears overflowing in her eyes.

"Keisha," she cried. "What have I done? Is my mom dead?"

Keisha took a deep breath. "You stabbed her, Chrissy! You stabbed her three times!"

"Did she make it?" Chrissy said. "Please tell me she did!" She looked as if she'd been crying the whole time she'd been there, her face sour and red.

"Yeah, Chrissy, she's in ICU, but she's gonna recover."

Chrissy let out a ragged sigh of relief, but the tears didn't stop.

"How could you do that to your own mother, Chrissy?"

"Keisha, I don't remember. I swear I don't remember any of it! I can't believe this is happening. What am I supposed to do about my baby?"

"You not getting off, Chrissy. You have to wait to see if the judge and jury grant you any leniency. You better pray like hell they do."

Keisha watched through the filthy glass as her friend sobbed uncontrollably. Chrissy begged for Keisha to have her back. She yelled for her to stick by her side. Keisha couldn't do anything but cry with her best friend after a while.

The guard informed Chrissy that her time was up. She headed back to her jail cell, and without a word, Keisha walked away. She knew she couldn't say or do anything. The fate of her best friend was now in the hands of the law.

****

After two months, court time had finally come. The judge and jury heard Chrissy's side of the story. Keisha even had to take the witness stand. Keith had disappeared and was nowhere to be found. And although Chrissy's mother was deeply hurt and had lost the use of her right arm, her demeanor on the witness stand clearly showed that she had forgiven her daughter.

The judge asked Chrissy, "Before sentencing, would you like to address the court?"

Chrissy stood up. "First of all, I would like to say that my emotions got the best of me. I am not a monster and I would never want to hurt my mom the way I did," she cried. "Mom, I truly apologize. I love you and I'm sorry for everything I've put you through. You were nothing but great to me. You didn't do anything to deserve this." She turned toward the judge. "I ask the court that you please place my daughter with my best friend Keisha Collins. Please don't make my baby suffer because of my actions. And please understand that if I could take back what I did, I would do so, without hesitation."

The judge looked at Chrissy.

"I haven't been a judge for many years. But I must admit that this is one case I will never forget. There is no justification for the crime you committed against your mother. You chose to deal with a man after finding out he was with your mother before he was with you. Not only was he with your mother, he was with a man as well. He lied to you, cheated on you, yet you stayed with him. You chose to get pregnant by this boy, because he's not a man, and you acted out of pure rage and jealousy. The state of Illinois hereby sentences you to the maximum sentence of twelve years in jail. You will get credit for time served and will be eligible for parole in eight years."

The gavel slammed down.

Keisha held Ms. Smith as they broke down in tears. The only good thing that came out of the hearing was that Keisha was granted custody of baby Breanne. It didn't stop Chrissy from crying.

As the bailiff led Chrissy out of the courtroom, she craned her neck toward her mom and best friend. "Keisha take care of Breanne! Mom, I'm sorry!"

They opened the doors and directed Chrissy through them.

Keisha and Ms. Smith headed home. As Keisha drove, she looked at Breanne's picture hidden in her sun visor. This wasn't the life she wanted for that girl, but it was the life they both were going to get.

You can follow the author on her social media sites:

Facebook

Kita Lashaun

Instagram

Kita_Lashaun

Favorite Quotes

"Find out who you are and do it on purpose."

--Dolly Parton

"If a person gets up after the fall, it is not physics, but character."

--Mike Tyson

"If you can't fly, then run.

If you can't run, then walk.

If you can't walk, then crawl.

But whatever you do you have to keep moving forward."

--Martin Luther King Jr.

"People only do to you what you allow. No one has the power, or authority, to pessimistically affect your existence unless you relinquish your rights to happiness."

--Kita LaShaun